AXEL STORM

JUNGLE FORTRESS

For all my friends in Guam

ORCHARD BOOKS
338 Euston Road, London NW1 3BH
Orchard Books Australia
Level 17/207 Kent Street, Sydney, NSW 2000

First published in 2010
First paperback publication in 2011

ISBN 978 1 40830 258 3 (hardback)
ISBN 978 1 40830 266 8 (paperback)

A CIP catalogue record for this book is available
from the British Library.

3

Printed in Great Britain

Orchard Books is a division of Hachette Children's Books,
an Hachette UK company.

AXEL STORM
JUNGLE FORTRESS

SHOO RAYNER

ORCHARD BOOKS

CHAPTER ONE

Axel Storm peeped over the railings
of his family's luxury yacht. He was
wearing mirrored wraparound
sunglasses and had pulled his hat
right down over his face.

A moment later, camera flashes from an army of photographers blazed away like machine guns.

"We're surrounded!" Axel gasped, crouching back down.

"What are we going to do about Axel?" his mum wailed. "Archie Flash, that horrid man from *Celebrity Gossip Magazine*, is here. He won't give up until he's got some photos of Axel."

Axel's mum and dad were rock stars. Their band, Stormy Skies, had recorded twenty-two platinum-selling hits in eighty-three different countries around the world.

They spent half their lives travelling, performing concerts and meeting their millions of fans. TV crews and newspaper photographers had lined the harbour to catch a glimpse of them.

"Sorry, Axel, but it looks like you'll have to stay below deck while we're here," Dad said. "We want you to grow up like any other normal boy. You can't be normal with your picture in the papers all the time."

"You mean we've sailed halfway across the world so I can be stuck on this stupid boat?" Axel moaned.

"It's hardly a boat, son," said Dad.

Stormy Ocean was the largest private yacht in the world!

It had a captain and ten sailors...

...five cooks, three maids *and* a butler.

It had a gym and two swimming pools...

...and a bowling alley.

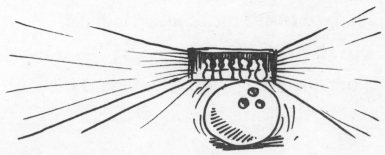

Not to mention a mini golf course...

...a 3D cinema...and a video games room!

"But I want to help you save the jungle!" Axel said. "I can't do that if I'm locked away on a floating prison."

Mum and Dad had sailed here to hold a massive rock concert in aid of saving the jungle. Thousands of Stormy Skies fans were coming to support them.

The jungle was under threat because Creesus Van Marbles, the head of the Van Marbles Burger Corporation, wanted more land for cows to make even more burgers for his restaurants. He planned to cut down all the trees in the jungle and grow grass instead!

Just then, something whistled through the air and shuddered into the wooden flagpole. *Twang-ang-ang!*

"What the...? It's a dart!" Dad yelped, ducking behind a sun lounger. "We're under attack!"

"There's a message wrapped around it," Axel hissed. He peeled the paper off and read it.

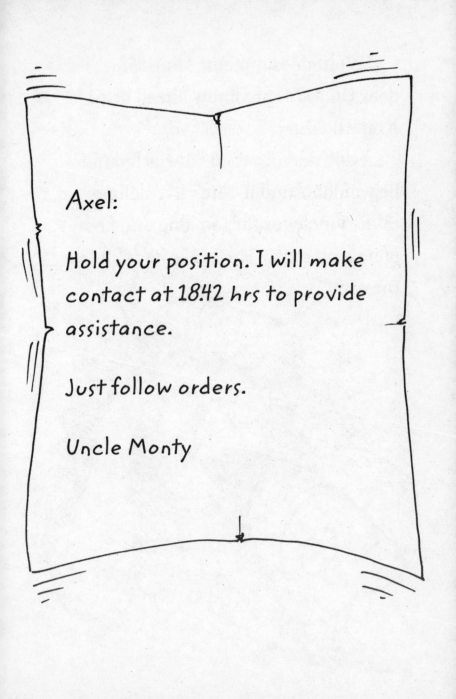

"What does it mean, Dad? How does Uncle Monty know I need help?" Axel asked.

Axel's dad groaned. "I was hoping he wouldn't find us! He's lived alone in the jungle for far too long and he's gone a bit crazy. He thinks he's still in the army!"

CHAPTER TWO

The sun faded and a crystal-clear, starry sky appeared over the harbour.

Axel checked his watch. "18.42," he muttered to himself.

"Psst!"

Axel looked around. The sound came from the water.

"Psst! Axel...over here! I'm coming on board."

Axel squinted into the gloom. A pair of eyes appeared in the darkness, staring wildly at him.

As if he was on patrol in a war zone, Uncle Monty dived over the rail, rolled across the deck and crouched, like a cat, beside a lifebelt. He wore combat clothes and his face was painted in camouflage cream.

"You can't be too careful," he whispered as he ruffled Axel's hair. "Good to see you, Axel. My, haven't you grown?"

Axel sighed. Why did his uncles always say that? He showed his uncle into the saloon, where his mum and dad were waiting.

"I've come all this way," Axel complained, "and because of Archie Flash I have to stay locked up on this boat! I wish I'd gone to Celebrity Kids' Club instead – and that's the worst thing in the world I can think of!"

"Axel will come and stay with me!"
Monty ordered. "I have a fortress so
I can defend the jungle from people like
Creesus Van Marbles. No one is going to
take pictures of Axel, I can assure you."

"Fortress?" Mum looked worried. "It
sounds a bit dangerous!"

"Oh, *Mum*, it sounds great! Please let
me… I'll die of boredom if I have to
stay here," moaned Axel.

"Don't worry," Uncle Monty said firmly. "I have everything he needs to survive in the jungle.

"Survive!" Mum squeaked. "That sounds even worse. I don't want Axel getting involved in any crazy adventures."

"He'll be safe with me," Uncle Monty said. He tossed a tin of camouflage cream over to Axel. "Here, Axel, put this on your face and we'll get going."

Three minutes later, Axel was dressed in dark clothes and his face was painted with the camouflage cream. He slid down the side of *Stormy Ocean* on a very thin rope.

Uncle Monty's boat was moored below. It was made from a hollowed-out tree trunk and was camouflaged with leafy branches.

"Keep your head down," Uncle Monty ordered. "If I paddle slowly, we'll look like an old log floating in the water. Once we're away from the photographers, I'll start the engine."

Axel looked up. Mum and Dad leant over the railings high above him.

"We love you Axel," they whispered. "Be good! See you after the concert."

"I'll be OK," Axel called. He smiled to himself – it felt like an adventure had started already!

CHAPTER THREE

Ocean Storm's comforting lights faded as Uncle Monty paddled the little boat upstream. "I think we're clear," Axel whispered. "I don't think anyone's following us."

"Right-ho!" Uncle Monty hissed. "I'll get the engine going. I've got blisters from all this paddling."

The full moon cast a ghostly glow. Endless trees lined the banks of the river. Axel began to relax under the twinkling stars...

Just then, a small inflatable boat appeared out of nowhere and swept across their bow.

"Hey! Watch out!" Axel shouted over the roar of the boat's powerful outboard motor.

Someone called his name. He peered into the gloom to see who was there. A dazzling light blinded him.

Oh no! It was Archie Flash, the *Celebrity Gossip Magazine* photographer. He would do anything to get a story about Axel.

"Where are you off to, then?" Archie yelled across the dark water.

"Go away, or we'll call the police!" Axel shouted.

Archie laughed. "Be my guest. The only law here is the Law of the Jungle!"

"He's right!" Uncle Monty muttered through gritted teeth.

Axel heard a *whoosh* as something shot across the water. With a loud bang and a long, slow hiss, Archie's inflatable boat began to sink under a mountain of bubbles.

"Help!" Archie squeaked.

"Mind the piranhas!" Uncle Monty called helpfully.

"What happened?" Axel asked.

"He must have been spying on you with a night-vision camera." Uncle Monty grinned. "He won't be following us any more. Inflatable boats are no use against blowpipe darts!"

"You punctured his boat?" Axel gasped.

"We don't want nosy parkers like him where we're going!" Uncle Monty said. "He can look after himself."

An hour later, Uncle Monty cut the engine and the little boat glided into a quiet creek that lay hidden behind overhanging branches.

"Welcome to my jungle fortress,"
Uncle Monty announced. "It was built
a thousand years ago. It was in ruins
before I discovered it."

The dark silhouette of a giant
pyramid rose above them. Axel could
hardly believe his eyes!

Uncle Monty led Axel past ancient carved pillars, down a dimly lit stone passage and through an open doorway. Beyond was a simple bedroom with two beds.

"This will keep the mosquitoes out," Uncle Monty said, pulling a net over Axel's bed. "Make sure it's tied down tight," he ordered. "It helps to keep the boa constrictors out, too!"

Then Uncle Monty placed a coil of something on a saucer and lit one end. Pale, yellow smoke drifted on the air.

"Urgh!" Axel complained. "That smells disgusting."

"It's meant to," Monty said, as he got into his own bunk. "The smoke repels insects, snakes, spiders and poisonous frogs. Night-night!" He was fast asleep and snoring before Axel could reply.

Axel snuggled into his sleeping bag and listened to the noises of the jungle night. He imagined he could hear all the snakes, spiders and poisonous frogs of the jungle, slithering and spinning and croaking around him – perhaps he should have gone to Celebrity Kids' Club after all!

CHAPTER FOUR

Axel woke to the smell of something utterly delicious. He fought his way out of the mosquito net and jumped out of his bunk.

The wonderful smell drew him to a room that looked like a laboratory. It was full of smoke and shiny metal equipment. Uncle Monty held a huge frying pan.

"Ah, good – you're awake," he smiled. "Hungry? Here, get this down you."

"Mmmm! These are delicious!" Axel said, waving a sausage around on his fork. "Are there any more?"

"Do you really like them?" Uncle Monty seemed pleased. He piled some onto Axel's plate. "There's plenty more where they came from."

While they ate, Uncle Monty told Axel all about his amazing fortress. "It was once an Inca temple," he explained. "I've made a few changes inside. It's my centre of operations – I control everything from here."

"What are you controlling?" Axel asked.

Uncle Monty pressed a button. A wall slid back to reveal a bank of screens.

"Cameras keep watch on the jungle and these screens track Creesus Van Marbles on the internet, via satellite," said Uncle Monty. "Van Marbles is ruthless – all he cares about is burgers. He'll cut down the jungle and everything I've worked for faster than you can say '*Timber*'! We have to be prepared."

"Prepared for what?" Axel asked.

"I'll show you, once you're kitted out for the jungle," Uncle Monty promised.

Soon, Axel was dressed in jungle camouflage. He had a carbon-fibre helmet on his head, a laser-guided blowpipe, a survival pack, and a pocket tool with fifty different attachments. Axel felt he was ready for anything.

"Make sure your trousers are
tucked into your boots," Uncle Monty
instructed. "You don't want leeches
getting in and sucking your blood!"

Yikes! Axel did exactly as he
was told.

"Follow me and don't do a thing
unless I tell you," Uncle Monty ordered.
"The jungle is a dangerous place!"

Uncle Monty knew the jungle like the back of his hand. He expertly led Axel along almost invisible animal tracks in the thick, leafy undergrowth.

"Look above you," Uncle Monty said, coming to a halt. Axel shrugged his shoulders. "They're just trees!" he said.

"Not any old trees." Uncle Monty reached up, picked a yellow fruit and gave it to Axel.

"It looks like a curled-up armadillo," Axel laughed.

Uncle Monty smiled. "That's why I call them armydillos! They are the most nutritious fruit in the world – one slice is equal to six portions of fruit and vegetables for a day. That's what your breakfast sausages were made from."

"What?" Axel's voice squeaked in surprise. "Fruit sausages?"

"I spent ten years in the Army Jungle Squad. The rations were terrible," Uncle Monty explained. "I decided to find a better way to feed soldiers. Armydillos are the answer. You can cook them in a million different ways."

Uncle Monty patted a tree trunk. "Armydillo trees only grow in this jungle. If Creesus Van Marbles cuts them all down, there will be no more armydillos – ever."

"That would be terrible," Axel gasped.

"It wouldn't just be the end of the armydillos," Uncle Monty continued. "It would be the end of the jungle and everything that lives in it."

"We have to stop him!" Axel said firmly.

"Indeed we do," said Uncle Monty. "But if you're going to help me foil Creesus Van Marbles' plans, my boy, you need some jungle training!"

"I'm ready when you are!" grinned Axel.

Axel spent the morning learning jungle survival techniques – and how to shoot a blowpipe!

"Put a dart in this end, aim the red laser spot at the target and blow as hard as you can," Uncle Monty said.

Axel's dart whistled out of the tube and slammed into the side of a tree.

"Good shot!" Uncle Monty cheered. "Blowpipes are the best weapon for jungle warfare."

"But – i-i-it's not really a war, i-i-is it, Uncle Monty?" Axel was worried now that he was so close to the front line!

"All I can tell you," his uncle said, "is that I will do anything to stop Creesus Van Marbles destroying the jungle."

Axel took a good look at his extraordinary uncle. "What exactly did you do in the army, Uncle Monty?" he asked.

"I was a cook!" he beamed. "One of the best. I won the All Army Master Chef competition!"

"So you're not really a deadly jungle assassin, then?" Axel said.

Uncle Monty looked surprised. "I never said I was!"

Just then, a string of tin cans began to jangle.

"Get down!" Uncle Monty hissed. "It's the alarm! We've got intruders!"

Axel held his breath. He felt his heart pounding in his chest. They were under attack!

It was soon obvious that the enemy
had not been to jungle training school.
They banged and crashed and cursed
and slashed their way through the
undergrowth. If they were going
to attack, they had lost the element
of surprise.

From his hiding place, Axel saw the
intruder standing with his back to them.

Axel loaded a dart into his blowpipe.
The red laser spot zeroed
in on the enemy's bottom.
Axel puffed as hard as
he could.

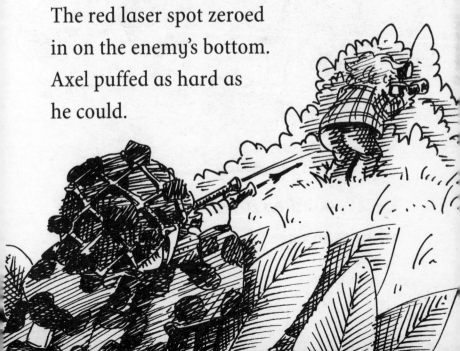

"YOWCH!" The enemy clutched his backside and hopped around the clearing as if he was on a trampoline.

Axel watched in horror as the ground rolled up and wrapped the intruder in a ball. He had hopped into one of Uncle Monty's traps! Now he dangled in the air like a fly in a giant spider's web.

"It's you!" Axel sighed, when he saw what they'd caught.

CHAPTER FIVE

Archie Flash was upside down, flapping in the net like a fish out of water. He did not look happy.

"Who do you work for?" Uncle Monty barked.

"Oh! Er! *Celebrity G-gossip M-magazine*, sir!" Archie stammered.

"And what's your mission?"

"T-to get photos of Axel, sir."

"Why?"

"It's my job, sir! Axel is the most famous celebrity child on the planet. Everybody wants to know what he's up to, sir." Archie waved his press card to prove who he was.

"So you have nothing to do with Creesus Van Marbles, then?

"No, sir!" Archie pleaded. "I don't like him at all. I'm all for saving the jungle, me, sir!"

When Archie was untangled and back on the ground, he stood to attention and saluted Uncle Monty.

"Were you ever in the army, Flash?"
Uncle Monty asked.

"Yes, sir!" Archie answered smartly.
"I drove tanks, sir."

Uncle Monty patted him on the
back. "Good man. I like your style and
determination. Shame you never did
jungle training!"

Back at the fortress, Archie rubbed some cream into his tender places and Uncle Monty served up sizzling-hot armydillo burgers.

"I'm sorry about your – er – um…"
Axel pointed at Archie's behind.
"I thought you were the enemy coming to cut down the trees."

"Don't worry about that! *Thif if the beft burger I've ever tafted!*" Archie spluttered through a mouthful of burger. "What is it?"

Uncle Monty explained how he had developed his armydillo recipes. "It's twice as nutritious as a beef burger," he explained.

"And twice as tasty!" Archie beamed.

Just then, the sound of chainsaws filled the air. Birds and monkeys fled shrieking through the jungle canopy as a giant tree creaked and groaned, then crashed to the ground not far away.

All around, the control panels lit up with one word – "Emergency!"

"Creesus has begun cutting down the trees. This means war!" Uncle Monty hissed. He looked Archie up and down. "Can you still drive a tank?"

CHAPTER SIX

Giant stone slabs scraped and screeched as they slid open to reveal a garage deep inside the jungle fortress.

Massive diesel engines bellowed out their deep, throaty roar as Archie drove the tank out into the sunshine.

"Wait! I've got an idea!" Axel rushed to the kitchen and scooped up a handful of armydillo burgers, then he scrambled up the side of the tank and dropped into the hatch on the turret.

"Forward, driver!" Uncle Monty yelled.

"Yes, sir!" Archie snapped back.

The tank crashed through the undergrowth, lurching towards their enemy.

Creesus Van Marbles himself was cutting down the first trees as a publicity stunt. Dressed in protective clothing and wielding an enormous chainsaw, he stood frozen in terror as Archie drove the tank towards him. The barrel of its enormous gun stopped one centimetre from Van Marble's polycarbonate protective visor!

The tank engine faltered and stopped. The chainsaw spluttered to a halt. A heavy silence descended on the jungle.

Axel popped his head out of the turret and held out an armydillo burger.

"Excuse me, Mr Van Marbles," he said in his most polite voice. "Would you like to try one of these?"

CHAPTER SEVEN

"I don't believe it!" said Dad.

Newspapers were spread all over the vast table in *Ocean Storm*'s saloon.

"Axel's only gone and saved the jungle on his own! They don't even mention our concert."

"There's a twenty-six page story about Axel in *Celebrity Gossip Magazine*," Mum sighed. "Look! There's a picture of him driving a tank with that horrible Archie Flash. He's never going to grow up like a normal boy if he carries on having these adventures."

"All I did was offer Mr Van Marbles an armydillo burger," Axel said. "And now that he knows how delicious they are, he doesn't want to cut down the trees! And anyway, Mr Flash is quite nice, really."

CREESUS VAN MARBLES became the vegetarian king today. He plans to open a chain of vegetarian restaurants called Armydillos.

"My good friend, Axel Storm, convinced me that armydillo burgers are not only good for you, but they taste better than any other burger on the planet," said Van Marbles.

Axel's uncle, Major Monty Storm, invented the armydillo burger hoping to save the jungle from destruction.

"THE ARMYDILLO MAY ALSO BE A CURE FOR THE COMMON COLD," an expert said.

When asked what he thought of his nephew, Major Storm said, "That boy's a deadly shot with a blowpipe!"

By ace reporter, Archie Flash.

SHOO RAYNER

ALL PRICED AT £3.99

Orchard Books are available from all good bookshops,
or can be ordered from our website: www.orchardbooks.co.uk,
or telephone 01235 827702, or fax 01235 827703.